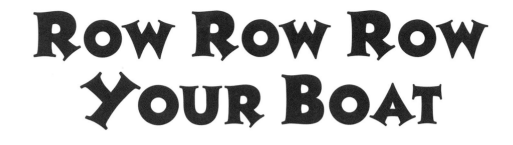

ROW ROW ROW YOUR BOAT

ROW ROW ROW YOUR BOAT

AS TOLD AND ILLUSTRATED BY
IZA TRAPANI

BEARBOAT
THE WOODS

WHISPERING COYOTE PRESS

Published by Whispering Coyote Press
300 Crescent Court, Suite 860, Dallas, TX 75201

Text was set in 18-point Tiffany Medium.
Book production and design by *The Kids at Our House*
10 9 8 7 6 5 4 3 2 1
Printed in the United States of America

Library of Congress Cataloging–in–Publication Data

Trapani, Iza.
Row Row Row Your Boat / written and illustrated by Iza Trapani.
p. cm.
Summary: Follows a family of bears on a fun-filled outing as their gentle boat ride
down the stream turns into a fast-paced adventure.
ISBN 1-58089-022-9
1. Children's songs—United States—Texas.   [1. Boats and boating—Songs and
music. 2. Songs.] I. Title.
PZ8.3.T686Ro 1999
782.42164'0268—dcE   dc21   98-50797
                                                                CIP
                                                                AC

For Pat and Margaret,
Johnny, Daniel, Helen, and Anna,
May you share many merry adventures!

Row row row your boat
Gently down the stream.
Merrily, merrily, merrily, merrily,
Life is but a dream.

Row row row your boat
Happy as can be
Sunshine glowing, off and rowing
With your family.

Row row row your boat
Stroke and follow through

Fumbling, flailing, oars go sailing—
What a clumsy crew!

Row row row your boat
Row with all your might

Rocking, bashing, water splashing
Better hold on tight!

Row row row your boat
Look ahead to find

Beavers damming, logging, jamming
Left you in a bind!

Row row row your boat
Stop to have a munch
Chomping, snacking, slurping, smacking
What a noisy bunch!

Row row row your boat
Better row to shore

Raining, hailing, wind is wailing
Hear the thunder roar!

Row row row your boat
Find a place that's dry
Scurry, scuttle, hide and huddle
Till the storm blows by.

Row row row your boat
And away you go

Skies are clearing, sunset nearing
Homeward bound you row.

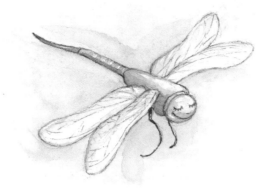

Row Row Row Your Boat

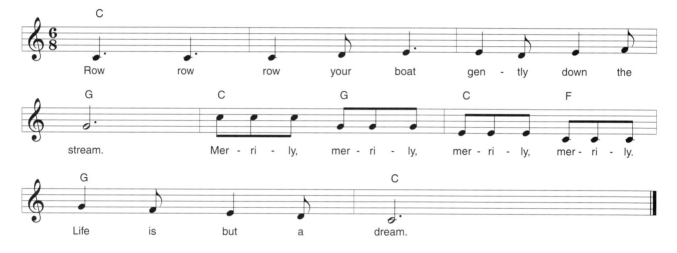

Row row row your boat gen-tly down the stream. Mer-ri-ly, mer-ri-ly, mer-ri-ly, mer-ri-ly. Life is but a dream.

2. Row row row your boat
   Happy as can be
   Sunshine glowing, off and rowing
   With your family.

3. Row row row your boat
   Stroke and follow through
   Fumbling, flailing, oars go sailing—
   What a clumsy crew!

4. Row row row your boat
   Row with all your might
   Rocking, bashing, water splashing
   Better hold on tight!

5. Row row row your boat
   Look ahead to find
   Beavers damming, logging, jamming
   Left you in a bind!

6. Row row row your boat
   Stop to have a munch
   Chomping, snacking, slurping, smacking
   What a noisy bunch!

7. Row row row your boat
   Better row to shore
   Raining, hailing, wind is wailing
   Hear the thunder roar!

8. Row row row your boat
   Find a place that's dry
   Scurry, scuttle, hide and huddle
   Till the storm blows by.

9. Row row row your boat
   And away you go
   Skies are clearing, sunset nearing
   Homeward bound you row.